Spring Garden
Sticker Storybook

Written by Guy Davis
Illustrated by Barry Goldberg

ISBN 0-439-69046-3
Designed by John Daly

First printing, March 2005
Reprinted by Scholastic India Pvt. Ltd., June 2006; September 2006; June 2014

Printed at Rave India, New Delhi

SCHOLASTIC INC.
New York   Toronto   London   Auckland   Sydney
New Delhi   Hong Kong

"Clifford, where are you?" calls Emily Elizabeth.

Emily Elizabeth is searching
for her little red puppy. Put Clifford
behind the wheelbarrow.

2

Emily Elizabeth wants to grow a garden outside her apartment building. "A beautiful garden will brighten everyone's day!" she says.

Clifford's furry friends like the idea of a garden, too. Place Flo and Zo next to Emily Elizabeth.

3

Emily Elizabeth takes Clifford to a garden supply center. "We need to start with seeds," she says.

Add seed packages to Emily Elizabeth's shopping basket.

"We also need gardening tools!" says Emily Elizabeth.

Clifford helps with the shopping!
Put a rake in his basket.

"Now we need to plant our seeds," says Emily Elizabeth.
"Let's start digging, Clifford!"

Place the shovel in Emily Elizabeth's hand.

Clifford loves digging!

Jorgé wants to dig in the dirt, too.
Put him next to Clifford so they both can dig.

"It's time to water our garden," says Emily Elizabeth.

Put the watering can next to Emily Elizabeth.

Norville will protect the seeds from the hungry pigeons.

Norville swoops to the rescue!
Add him flying above the garden.

9

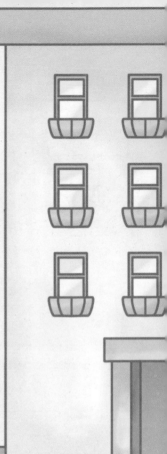

"We've planted and watered our seeds," says Emily Elizabeth. "Now the sun will help them grow!"

Place the sun in the sky.

10

Everyone takes a break in the sunshine.

Daffodil can't wait for the carrots to grow!
Put her next to the carrot patch.

11

"Look, Clifford!" says Emily Elizabeth.
"Our seedlings have sprouted!"

Add more seedlings to
the empty garden rows.

"Now it's time to pull out the weeds," says Emily Elizabeth.

The caterpillar is hungry.
Place him on a weed so he can eat.

A few weeks later, the garden is in full bloom!

Add flowers between Flo and Zo.

"These flowers smell so good!" says Emily Elizabeth.

*Put Clifford next to Emily Elizabeth
so that he can smell the flowers.*

Many living creatures share the garden.

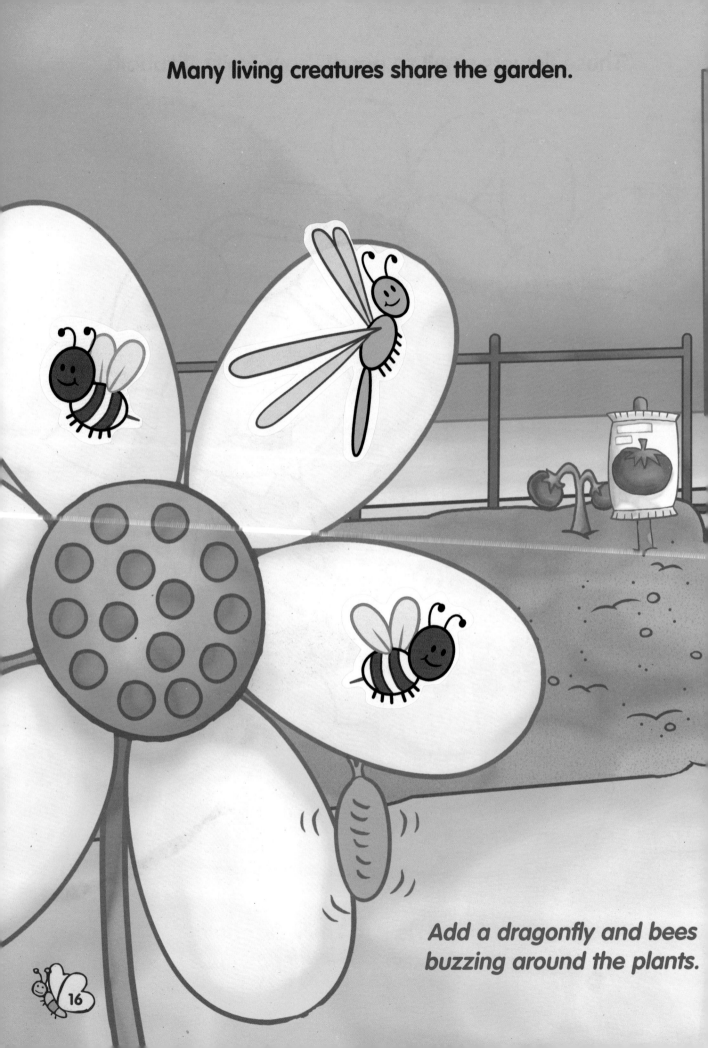

Add a dragonfly and bees
buzzing around the plants.

16

"Good boy, Clifford!" says Emily Elizabeth.
"The carrots are ready to eat!"

Put a bunch of carrots next to Daffodil.

It's harvest time! Emily Elizabeth picks ripe, red strawberries!

Put more strawberries in Emily Elizabeth's basket.

The caterpillar changes into a beautiful butterfly!

Put more butterflies flying around the garden.

**"I love having fresh flowers to give my friends!"
says Emily Elizabeth.**

Give Nina flowers from Emily Elizabeth.

20

One tomato will feed the whole Sidarsky family!

Give the Sidarskys a [tomato to eat.]

All the neighbors love
the beautiful garden!

Mr. Howard gave Emily Elizabeth
a bird feeder. Put it in the garden.

"Our garden had all the right ingredients," says Emily Elizabeth. "Seeds, dirt, sun, water . . . and lots of love!"

Place Clifford in the middle of the garden.

"Thanks for all your help, Clifford," says Emily Elizabeth.
"Our garden has made everyone happy!"

The city birds love the garden, too!
Place birds around the bird feeder.

24